Myrtle, Tertle and Gertle

Also by Emma Chichester Clark
CATCH THAT HAT!
LISTEN TO THIS
(Compiled by Laura Cecil)
STUFF AND NONSENSE
(Compiled by Laura Cecil)
THE STORY OF
HORRIBLE HILDA AND HENRY

for
Luke

A Red Fox Book

Published by Random Century Children's Books
20 Vauxhall Bridge Road, London SW1V 2SA

A division of the Random Century Group
London Melbourne Sydney Auckland
Johannesburg and agencies throughout the world

First published by The Bodley Head Ltd 1989

Red Fox edition 1992

ISBN 0 09 987130 0

Myrtle, Tertle and Gertle

Emma Chichester Clark

Tertle   Gertle   Myrtle

RED FOX

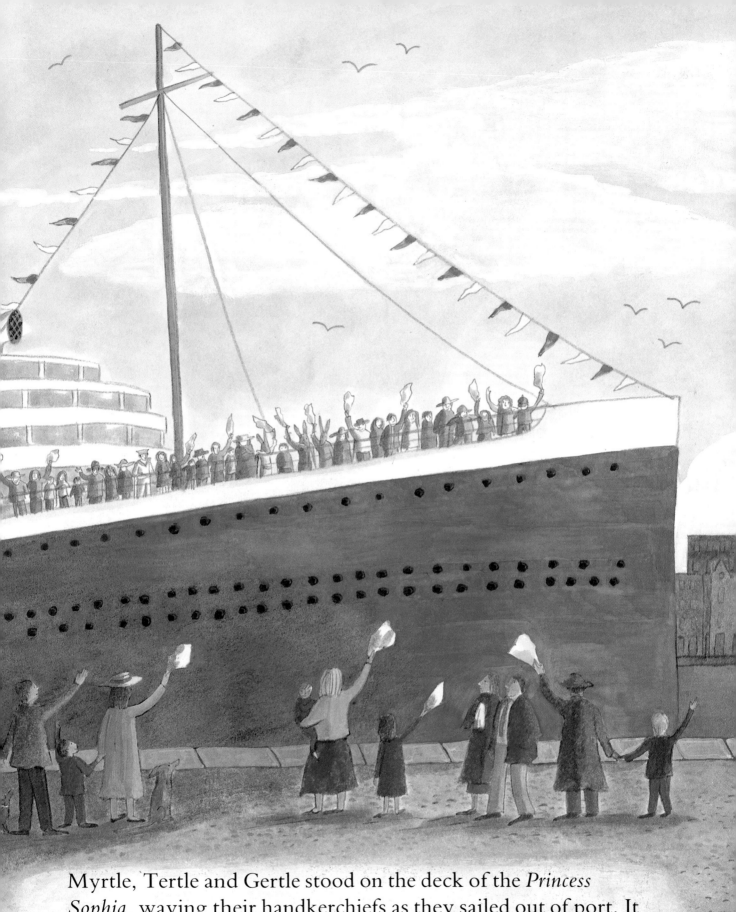

Myrtle, Tertle and Gertle stood on the deck of the *Princess Sophia*, waving their handkerchiefs as they sailed out of port. It was the beginning of their summer holiday.

After they had unpacked, they went up on deck to look at the view. Gertle leaned recklessly over the rail to look at a passing seagull.

That evening the Captain invited them to sit at his table for dinner, and afterwards they slept soundly in their bunks as the ship sailed through the night.

The next day there were games on the sun-deck. They played quoits against Mrs Brackenbury and her poodle, Pom-Pom, but Gertle wasn't very good at it.

After a tug-of-war with the sailors, there followed a rigorous programme of exercises.

A few days later, they visited an island where there were lots of little houses and cats. Pom-Pom was afraid of cats, so Mrs Brackenbury held on to her tightly.

While the others looked at ruined temples which had been built long ago, Gertle talked to the goats.

Then they went to a museum full of pots and statues. Gertle found it all very tiring, so she found a chair in the shade, where she closed her eyes and fell asleep. Nobody noticed she had gone.

She slept until it was dark and only woke up when she heard the ship's horn in the harbour.

She ran as fast as she could, but when she got to the quayside, it was too late. The *Princess Sophia* had gone and she was left behind.

Gertle was very frightened. She climbed into a little boat that was tied up at the quayside and bravely began to row out to sea in search of the *Princess Sophia*.

Gertle rowed all night, and when the sun came up the next morning, she had no idea where she was.

She found a sandwich in her pocket that she had saved from the day before,

...bow wow wow wooooooow...

but just as she was eating it, she heard a strange crying coming from the water behind her.

She looked over the back of the boat, and there, to her great surprise, was Pom-Pom! The poor little poodle had fallen overboard from the *Princess Sophia* and was quite exhausted from swimming.

Gertle lifted her to safety into the boat.

As they rowed on, the sea became rougher and the wind blew the waves higher and higher.

There was a terrible storm. Gertle and Pom-Pom held tightly to the boat as the waves tossed it up and down relentlessly. They were both very cold and frightened. Water was pouring into the boat and Gertle was afraid they would sink.

When the boat finally turned over, Pom-Pom was too tired to swim any more. Gertle held on to her collar and kept her head above water, as they swam back to the up-turned boat.

Meanwhile Myrtle, Tertle and Mrs Brackenbury were on the deck of the *Princess Sophia* desperately searching for Gertle and Pom-Pom. Suddenly they saw them through Tertle's telescope and alerted the Captain. The ship sent up a flare and Gertle and Pom-Pom knew they were saved at last.

Myrtle and Tertle went in the lifeboat to rescue Gertle and Pom-Pom.

"Oh Gertle," they said. "We are so proud of you. You have saved the life of Mrs Brackenbury's poodle, and you are safe and sound!"

The lifeboat was hoisted up the side of the ship. The
passengers cheered and threw flowers. Gertle, the heroine, was
safe. Pom-Pom barked and barked, and Mrs Brackenbury shed
a tear of relief.

There were huge celebrations back on board the *Princess Sophia*. Everyone congratulated Gertle on her bravery and the Captain awarded her a medal for courage and stamina in adversity and for the rescue of Mrs Brackenbury's poodle.

Some bestselling Red Fox picture books

THE BIG ALFIE AND ANNIE ROSE STORYBOOK
by Shirley Hughes
OLD BEAR
by Jane Hissey
JOHN PATRICK NORMAN MCHENNESSY –
THE BOY WHO WAS ALWAYS LATE
by John Burningham
I WANT A CAT
by Tony Ross
NOT NOW, BERNARD
by David McKee
THE STORY OF HORRIBLE HILDA AND HENRY
by Emma Chichester Clark
THE SAND HORSE
by Michael Foreman and Ann Turnbull
BAD BORIS GOES TO SCHOOL
by Susie Jenkin-Pearce
MRS PEPPERPOT AND THE BILBERRIES
by Alf Prøysen
BAD MOOD BEAR
by John Richardson
WHEN SHEEP CANNOT SLEEP
by Satoshi Kitamura
THE LAST DODO
by Ann and Reg Cartwright
IF AT FIRST YOU DO NOT SEE
by Ruth Brown
THE MONSTER BED
by Jeanne Willis and Susan Varley
DR XARGLE'S BOOK OF EARTHLETS
by Jeanne Willis and Tony Ross
JAKE
by Deborah King